GARFIELD

THE
EASTER BUNNY?

Published by Grosset & Dunlap, Inc., a member of The Putnam Publishing Group, New York.
Published simultaneously in Canada. Printed in the U.S.A.
Library of Congress Catalog Card Number: 88-80513   ISBN 0-448-09297-2
A B C D E F G H I J

GARFIELD

THE
EASTER BUNNY?

Created by
JIM DAVIS

Written by Jim Kraft

Publishers • Grosset & Dunlap • New York

"Tomorrow is Easter, boys," said Jon Arbuckle to Garfield the cat and Odie the dog. "We've got to get ready for the Easter Bunny."

Garfield and Odie watched excitedly as Jon took three Easter baskets from the closet and set them on the table. There was one basket for each of them.

Garfield looked at his basket and frowned. "My basket is much too small," he said. "I want something about the size of a bathtub."

"When we wake up tomorrow," said Jon, "these baskets will be filled with treats."

"By the time you wake up, my tummy will be filled with your treats," thought Garfield with a sly grin.

Jon and Odie went off to bed. But Garfield didn't want to miss the Easter Bunny. The clock struck one, and then two. Garfield's tummy was getting impatient.

"If the Easter Bunny doesn't come soon," he thought, "I'll have to send out for pizza."

Suddenly he saw the shadow of two big floppy ears.

"The Easter Bunny!" cried Garfield.

Garfield grabbed his Easter basket. "Fill it up!" he said. "Gimme candy, candy, and more candy!"

"Arf?" said a familiar voice.

"Oh, it's only you, Odie," said Garfield sadly.

Odie bounded into the room, wagging his tail and his tongue.

"Did you come to keep me company, old friend?" asked Garfield.

Odie shook his head.

"Did you come because you don't trust me with your candy?" said Garfield.

"Arf!" said Odie.

"For a dumb dog, you're pretty smart," said Garfield.

Odie settled down beside Garfield and was soon fast asleep.

When the clock struck three, and the Easter Bunny had still not arrived, Garfield decided he couldn't wait any longer.

"Wake up," he said, tugging on Odie's ear. "The Easter Bunny must be lost. We'll have to go out and look for him."

"Arf," said Odie in agreement. So he and Garfield crept out of the house into the night.

"This is a job for your nose, Odie," said Garfield. "See if you can sniff out the Easter Bunny."

Odie tried hard. But after an hour, all he managed to track down was a fire hydrant and an old bunny slipper.

"Guess I'll have to find the Easter Bunny myself," said Garfield. "Let's see. If I were the Easter Bunny, where would I be right now?"

"Home in bed, if you were smart," said a strange voice.

Garfield and Odie spun around. There, slumped against a streetlamp, was the Easter Bunny himself!

"Where have you been?" said Garfield. "My tummy was expecting you hours ago!"

"From the looks of your tummy, it could use a little rest," said the Easter Bunny.

"This is one crabby Easter Bunny," Garfield said to Odie.

"I'm sorry," said the Easter Bunny. "But you'd be crabby, too, if you had my job. My back is sore from carrying this heavy basket and my feet are killing me, and I'm not even halfway through with my deliveries. And why do I bother? Santa Claus gets all the attention. Nobody really cares about the Easter Bunny. I think I'll just quit right now."

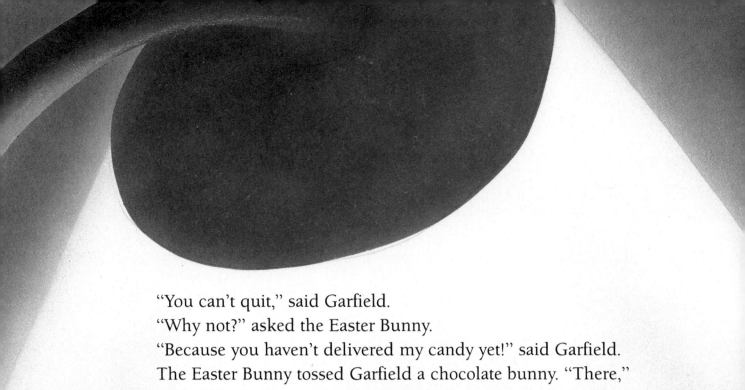

"You can't quit," said Garfield.

"Why not?" asked the Easter Bunny.

"Because you haven't delivered my candy yet!" said Garfield.

The Easter Bunny tossed Garfield a chocolate bunny. "There," he said. "Happy Easter. Now, go away."

"You're going to make a lot of kids very unhappy," said Garfield.

"What can I do?" said the Easter Bunny. "I'm pooped. This job is just too much for one rabbit."

"It doesn't look so hard to me," said Garfield. "After all, you work only one night a year."

"If you think you can handle the job," said the tired rabbit, "then you be the Easter Bunny."

"Anything a bunny can do, a cat can do better!" said Garfield.

The Easter Bunny gave Garfield a pair of bunny ears. "You'll need to wear these," he said.

"Do I have to?" asked Garfield.

"It's the official uniform," said the Easter Bunny.

Then the Easter Bunny handed Garfield a large basket filled with Easter treats to deliver.

"Wow! Look at all this tasty loot!" said Garfield.

"No eating on the job," said the Easter Bunny. "Now you'd better get going. You've got to finish before morning."

"No problem," said Garfield. "I'll show you how easy your job is."

The Easter Bunny didn't say anything. He only closed his eyes and smiled.

So Garfield, the Easter Bunny, went off to deliver his Easter goodies with his trusty assistant, Odie.

They hadn't gone far before Garfield discovered that the basket of goodies was, indeed, very, very heavy.

"This thing weighs more than I do," said Garfield. "We need to lighten the load, and I know just the way to do it!"

Garfield began eating the Easter candy in the basket.

"Arf, arf!" said Odie, shaking his paw at Garfield.

"Relax," said Garfield. "There's still plenty of candy left."

Garfield and Odie arrived at the first house. "Let's get to work," said Garfield. But then he stopped. "How does the Easter Bunny get inside?" he wondered. "I never thought about that!"

Garfield tried the front door, but of course it was locked. The back door was locked, too.

"Arf!" said Odie, pointing to the chimney.

"Wrong holiday, Odie," said Garfield.

Finally Garfield found an open basement window. Unfortunately, it was too small a window for such a very fat cat. Garfield got stuck!

"Give me a push, Odie!" he cried.

Odie pushed, but Garfield didn't budge. "Push harder!" said Garfield.

Odie backed up, gritted his teeth, lowered his head, and charged full speed into Garfield. *SMACK!* Garfield popped through the window and landed *FOOMP!* in a basket of laundry.

"Maybe this job isn't so easy after all," he thought. "I still have to find the Easter baskets. Fortunately, cats can see in the dark."

Garfield climbed out of the laundry basket and ran straight into a table leg. "Unfortunately," he said, "we can see only if we use a flashlight!"

Two seconds later Garfield stepped on a toy car and his feet flew out from under him. Easter eggs went rolling all around the room. He was barely able to squeeze out of the house before the people came downstairs to see about the noise!

"That was rough," said Garfield. "I need a candy break."

Garfield and Odie turned a corner and came face to face with a pack of big mean dogs, who looked hungrily at the fat bunny and his basket of treats.

"Here's the plan, Odie," Garfield whispered. "RUUUUUN!"

They ran for their lives, scrambling under hedges and over fences, with the dogs snarling at their heels! And the whole time the Easter goodies were flying out of Garfield's basket!

"Whose idea was it to take this job?" Garfield said, panting.

Odie pointed at Garfield and kept right on running.

The dogs decided to stop and eat all of the candy Garfield had dropped. After a while Garfield and Odie realized that they were no longer being chased. With their hearts pounding, they flopped on the ground.

"The Easter Bunny must be in great shape," Garfield gasped.

Though they were bruised and exhausted, Garfield and Odie weren't ready to quit. But it was nearly morning. They needed a fast way to deliver the rest of the treats!

"I've got it!" said Garfield. "We'll stack the treats outside the door and ring the bell. People will come out, find the treats, and fill their own baskets. It will be a self-serve Easter!" Garfield put his plan into action— and it worked!

"We did it, Odie!" said Garfield as the sun came up. "Thanks to us, everyone will have Easter treats! Everyone…except…Oh, no! We did too good a job. We forgot to leave some treats for ourselves!"

Odie howled with disappointment.

But when Garfield and Odie got home, their Easter baskets were overflowing with treats!

"Tah-dah!" Up popped the Easter Bunny! "I thought you deserved a reward," he said. "You've had a rough night."

"How do you know?" asked Garfield.

"I followed you," said the Easter Bunny. "Now you see what a tough job I have."

"You're right," said Garfield. "It's tough, even for a brilliant cat like me. Tell me," he continued, nibbling a chocolate bunny, "how do you get inside people's houses, anyway?"

"Let's just say I use a little Easter Bunny magic," said the Easter Bunny with a wink. "But since you're so good at delivering things, maybe you'd like to help me out again next year."

"No way," said Garfield. "From now on, the only bunny I want to see is a chocolate one!"